I0712754

FROM THE WORLD OF OLD GRANDMOTHER'S TREE

Dance of Creation

VOLUME 3

JOSEPH BOLTON

ILLUSTRATED BY NATASHA PELLEY-SMITH

Augustine's Alley

Cover design and illustrations by Natasha Pelley-Smith
Interior book design by the Aaxel Author Group
www.aaxelauthorgroup.com

ISBN (Hardback): 979-8-9853588-5-8
ISBN (Paperback): 979-8-9892325-8-1
ISBN (eBook): 979-8-9892325-9-8

This is a work of fiction. Miteouamigoukoue and Father Elisée Crey mentioned in this book are historical persons who lived in 17th century Québec. Other names, characters, events and incidents are the products of the author's imagination. Any resemblance to actual persons, living or dead, or actual events is purely coincidental.

Publisher's Cataloging-in-Publication Data
provided by Five Rainbows Cataloging Services

Names: Bolton, Joseph, 1964- author. | Pelley-Smith, Natasha, illustrator.
Title: Dance of creation : from the world of old grandmother's tree / Joseph Bolton.
Description: Leominster, MA : Augustine's Alley, 2025. | Series: Old grandmother's tree, vol. 3.
Identifiers: ISBN 979-8-9892325-8-1 (paperback) | ISBN 979-8-9892325-9-8 (ebook)
Subjects: LCSH: Indigenous peoples--Canada--Folklore. | Indigenous peoples--Folklore--Social aspects. | Creation--Folklore. | Storytelling. | Short stories. | Illustrated works. | BISAC: FICTION / Indigenous / Oral Storytelling & Teachings. | FICTION / World Literature / Canada / General. | FICTION / Short Stories (single author) | FICTION / Indigenous / Oral Storytelling & Teachings. | GSAFD: Folklore.
Classification: LCC PS3602.O48 D35 2025 (print) | LCC PS3602.O48 (ebook) | DDC 813/.6--dc23

This book is proudly sponsored by the Leominster Massachusetts Cultural Council.

In remembrance of my younger brother Patrick Bolton,
whom I carried in my arms when he was a baby.

1970–2023

Introduction

"Miteouamigoukoue lived a full life with dignity, respect, and love.
A courageous and loving Algonquin [woman]."

—Father Elisée Crey, Récollet Priest,
Pastor of Trois-Rivières, Québec,
January 1699

Father Elisée Crey's eulogy of my Algonquin ancestor Miteouamigoukoue is at the heart of the *Old Grandmother's Tree* series. Written with clarity and brevity, it beautifully honors a life marked by dignity, respect, love, and courage. I dare say it is the most effective eulogy ever written.

For a 17th century Canadian priest to write so well on the passing of a woman is remarkable. It is even more remarkable considering that Miteouamigoukoue was a 17th century First Nations—not European—woman. His words reveal that Miteouamigoukoue overcame great personal tragedy, was respected by both the Algonquin and French communities, showed kindness, leadership, courage and faith, and valued dignity. I also believe that Father Crey and Miteouamigoukoue were friends. That friendship will play a key part in the upcoming Volume 4 of the *Old Grandmother's Tree* series.

Father Crey's words are a treasured gift to the thousands of Miteouamigoukoue's descendants in Canada and the United States. We also owe a debt to fellow Miteouamigoukoue descendant Normand Léveillée (1935-2019), whose research rescued the records of Miteouamigoukoue's life from obscurity. After he passed away, his website was closed, but I was able to secure most of his research before it was lost forever, and it is now available on the Old Grandmother's Tree website.

Immersing myself deeply in the life of Miteouamigoukoue inspired me to connect with Algonquin communities in Canada, as I did when I visited Magog, Quebec in August 2022. An Internet search led to a trip to Pembroke, Ontario in July 2024 and a visit with Paul Laderoute, Administrator/Designate of the Algonquins of Greater Golden Lake First Nation.

Paul subsequently introduced me to other Miteouamigoukoue descendants living in Pembroke, and later to Joanne Haskin, Executive Director, of the Mashkiwizii Manido Foundation. Joanne Haskin and other members of the Foundation warmly received me when I returned to visit later that year in November, It was the first time I made connections with the people and culture of my ancestor Miteouamigoukoue.

I wish to thank Paul Laderoute, Joanne Haskin, Trevor Pearce (who is a Miteouamigoukoue descendant), Margaret Haskin, Julianna Morin and many others from the unceded, ancestral territory of the Algonquin Anishinaabe Nation in and around Pembroke Ontario for welcoming me into their families. I am happy to include the Algonquin communities in this story and to know that Miteouamigoukoue's spirit of dignity, love, respect, courage, faith and resiliency is thriving in Pembroke.

Dance of Creation is the third volume of the *Old Grandmother's Tree* series and, as you will discover, is both a sequel and a prequel to the stories in Volumes 1 and 2. Please note that Waaseyaa in this story is the same character as Géant Poilu from Volume 2. Poor Jacques LaRue was totally confused by his encounter with Waaseyaa and never bothered to stay in his company long enough to learn his proper name. Jacques LaRue could only describe Waaseyaa's appearance to the equally befuddled residents of Saint-Honoré, Québec.

While Volumes 1 and 2 were written in the language of a folktale, this book is written as a creation mythology story. This story is all original to me, but I wrote it in the spirit and tradition of Creation Mythologies of First Nations and, to a lesser extent, mythological stories from around the world. I know that you will enjoy this book and will pass it on to others. More than ever, we need good stories to tell around the campfire.

I wish to again thank Alexa Nazzaro of the Aaxel Author Group and our storyboard artist, Masami Kiyono who, in addition to creating rough sketches for this book, provided great suggestions for the story. Everywhere I go with the *Old Grandmother's Tree* books, the very first thing that everyone says is, "Oh, what beautiful illustrations! Who did them?" At that point, I will happily brag about artist Natasha Pelley-Smith and her magical illustrations full of depth, color and character. Thank you, Natasha, for hanging with me for "just one more story." Enjoy those illustrations! Natasha worked very hard on them.

See you all next year for Volume 4 as the remarkable story of Miteouamigoukoue comes to a dramatic and heartfelt conclusion.

Joseph Bolton
August 2025

Mont-St-Hilaire
Les Créateurs
Les frères & Sœurs
De Waaseyaa & Mikcheech
Mont Orford
Lac Magog
Bolton Centre
Mont Sutton
Lac Memphrémagog
Mikcheech
Le Géant de Montagne Tremblant
Fleuve Saint-Laurent
Québec
Waaseyaa
Memphré
Lac Memphrémagog

Pembroke, Ontario, Canada
Wednesday night, August 7, 2126

An Algonquin grandfather is camping with his grandchildren ...

My grandchildren, come, sit here with me under the stars and
around this warm fire, for I have a story to tell you. It is a story that
has been passed down to me by my grandparents, who received it
from their grandparents, and who in turn received it
from their grandparents.

The story begins this way:

It was the moment before all other moments, and the dream before all other dreams. The Creator danced into existence a beautiful World for his People in which to live in peace, harmony and love.

But before any of the People walked the land, the Creator called forth a family of beings to be the People's Elder Brothers and Elder Sisters. The Creator gave each of these Elder Brothers and Elder Sisters a gift that they could use to help the People.

The first of the Elder Beings to be created were Waaseyaa the Giant, whose name means First Light from the Rising Sun, and his brother, Mikcheech the Turtle. They are the Elder Brothers of all the Elder Beings that followed.

As the eldest brother, Waaseyaa was given the gift of wisdom so he could help his younger brothers and sisters. He was also given a share in the Creator's power to call forth living beings.

When Waaseyaa's younger brother Mikcheech was born, the Creator kissed him and also gave him a gift. Mikcheech's gift is that when he meets a human being, he can see the Creator's dance that brought that person to life. Each dance is different for each person, and through it, Mikcheech can see the talents and gifts that make that person unique.

Did you all know that before we sat down together tonight? Think how wonderful it is: At the moment that you were born, the Creator danced a joyful dance, a dance that is unique and different for each of you. Mikcheech can see that dance if he meets you. That is his gift.

Next, the Creator brought forth the younger sisters of Waaseyaa
and Mikcheech. First was their sister Wenona the Orca. Her name
means First Born Daughter and her gift is to be the special protector
of mothers.

Next was their sister Namid the Snowy Owl. Her name means
Star Dancing and her gift is the ability to bring the power of the stars
down to the Earth to protect the People from evil
magic and mischief.

Namid was followed by Bawaajige the Polar Bear and her name
means Dreams. The Creator gave her control of the People's dreams.
Did you ever awaken from a dream, remembering the warmth
and the happiness of a magical place in your deepest imagination?
Perhaps you remember a dream that gave you courage and
inspiration? Those dreams are the gift from Bawaajige.

The youngest were their brothers Shkaabewis the Caribou who is
known as Helper of the Medicine People, and Animkii the Bald Eagle
who, as his name Thunder implies, brings the rain, thunder and
lightning to the World.

Waaseyaa and his three younger brothers and three younger sisters
are known as the Elder Beings, since they came before all other
living things.

After the Elder Beings, the Creator called forth other mysterious creatures, like the giants who rule over the mountains and the magical Lake Monsters who guard the largest lakes of the World.

After all of them, the Creator placed the animals, fish, birds and all the living things that we see around us. Lastly, seeing that the World was good, the Creator created human beings, who we refer to as the People.

The Creator could see that the People did not know how to fashion the things that they needed to live, and they did not know how to live in peace with each other.

So, out of love for the People, the Creator asked Waaseyaa and his brothers and sisters to find the People and teach them so that they could be happy.

Following the Creator's command, the Elder Beings all started to run towards the People who were now in the World. As they were running, Waaseyaa could see that his younger brother, Mikcheech the Turtle, could not keep up with the rest of their brothers and sisters. What did Waaseyaa do? Well, he stopped, turned around, picked up Mikcheech and
put him on his shoulder.

GRAHAM
CRACKER

Why did Waaseyaa wait for his younger brother, Mikcheech? Because that is what older brothers and sisters do for their younger brothers and sisters. This was the first lesson that, through his example, Waaseyaa taught the People.

Seeing that they could not catch up with their brothers and sisters, who were now far ahead of them, Waaseyaa and Mikcheech decided to follow their own path to explore the new World and to find People to help.

Now, this time was so long ago that the Great Ice that had once covered the land had only just begun to retreat back to the north.

After a few days' journey, the brothers arrived at a village that will, in the many years to come, become known as Trois Rivières. In this ancient village, they discovered that an Elder Being known as Lugubre was tormenting the People.

Who is this Lugubre, you may ask? She is also an Elder Being and a child of the Creator. However, before I go on to the next part of the story, I must tell you something important. What you need to know is that the Creator gave all his children the gift of free will. They can choose to serve and love the People and the Creator or not. It is frightening that living beings can choose evil and misery of their own free will. It is the most powerful and dangerous of all the Creator's gifts because it is so easy to misuse.

Lugubre became jealous when she saw how much the Creator loved the People, even though the Creator loved her as well. She resented that the Creator asked her to serve the People, whom she saw as inferior to her. In her pride, she believed that she was the greatest of all the Creator's children and that everyone in the World should obey her. Sadly, her choice to turn away from the Creator's love left her angry and unhappy.

When she found some of the People, she decided to teach them the ways of selfishness, unkindness and the destruction of the beautiful World that the Creator gave them. Why did she do this? She believed that if the People lived in fear and anger, they would be subservient to her. But above all else, Lugubre wanted the People to be as miserable as she was.

Waaseyaa and Mikcheech confronted Lugubre and told her that she was not teaching the People the ways of the Creator. Lugubre pointed out that because the People were willingly listening to her, she had a right to be there.

The brothers responded that the People did not understand who Lugubre was, and that they had to be free to choose whom to follow. They told her she could leave on her own, or they would remove her from the village.

Lugubre thought about challenging Waaseyaa and Mikcheech, but she could see the power of their wisdom and of the love in their hearts. That power confused and frightened her. Since Lugubre is a bully and all bullies cower in fear in the face of strength, she ran away.

With Lugubre gone from the village, Waaseyaa and Mikcheech looked towards the People. They could see that they did not know how to live. So, the two Elder Beings decided to stay and help and teach them.

Waaseyaa taught them how to build long houses and fires to stay warm.

Mikcheech taught the People to be kind and to live in peace with each other. He also taught them medicine so they could heal themselves, and he gave them stories to pass on to their children and their grandchildren.

Perhaps this story that I am telling you now was first told by Mikcheech around a campfire just like this one.

Although Waaseyaa and Mikcheech drove away Lugubre, she watched the village from afar with jealousy and plotted her revenge.

Stretching forth her hands, Lugubre fashioned Ice Giants from rock, ice and wood. Their edges were sharp, and within the transparent ice you could see logs, dirt and boulders that helped to give their bodies form and strength.

How could she create these Ice Giants, you ask? Remember how I told you that when they were born, all of the Creator's children were given a gift to use to serve the People? It was the same for Lugubre as well. Her gift is that she is able to fashion beautiful works of art from rock, dirt, wood and ice. She was given this gift so that she could use it to help and to teach the People.

Even though she turned away from the Creator, she still had this gift because the Creator does not take back the gifts given to his children, even if they misuse them.

But because the heart of Lugubre turned away from the Creator, her gift became distorted and twisted. Now she can only create ugly and destructive things, like the cold and lifeless Ice Giants, who were now marching relentlessly towards the village. Lugubre wanted to use the Ice Giants to frighten and punish the People into obedience to her.

The People ran in terror, but Mikcheech bravely stood his ground, while his brother Waaseyaa found a log to use as a club and went on the attack.

The Ice Giants shattered from the blows of Waaseyaa while Mikcheech stood firm in front of the People, protecting them and giving them courage. After a hard-fought battle, the crumbling and shattered Ice Giants began to melt.

Two of the Ice Giants that melted became a great river that the People called Magtogoek. The French call this river Fleuve Saint-Laurent.

One of the Ice Giants, however, melted into a pond that Mikcheech took as his home. The nose of that Ice Giant rested in the center of this pond as a large rock.

In the years that followed, Mikcheech enjoyed sleeping on this rock while soaking in the warmth of Grandfather Sun. It also made Mikcheech happy to know that by sitting on that rock, he was placing his turtle butt on top of the melted face of one of Lugubre's fierce Ice Giants.

Lugubre never forgave this insult of seeing Waaseyaa and Mikcheech defeat her Ice Giants. She watched in frustration and rage as the People began to live in peace with each other by following the teachings of Waaseyaa and Mikcheech.

Lugubre hated them for siding against her, but she was patient. She believed that the People would eventually forget the ways of Waaseyaa and Mikcheech and would again be vulnerable to her evil ways. In fact, she did return again thousands of years later to try to destroy the People of Trois-Rivières in revenge. But that is a story for another night, around another campfire.

After defeating the Ice Giants, Waaseyaa and his brother Mikcheech remained with the People at Trois-Rivières, teaching and helping them for many years.

However, Waaseyaa, remembering that the Creator wished that they help other People as well, decided that he and Mikcheech should continue on their journey through the World.

The People, however, felt sad and worried when they realized that Waaseyaa and his brother Mikcheech were going to leave them, and they begged them to stay. At the same time, Mikcheech came to see the People as his children, and he asked his brother if he could stay with them. Reluctantly, Waaseyaa agreed to allow Mikcheech to stay and so Waaseyaa said goodbye to his brother, whom he would miss very much.

Alone for the first time in his life, Waaseyaa sought out other People to help and to teach. He missed his brother Mikcheech, and he missed his other brothers and sisters, whom he had not seen since the beginning of the World. He wondered if they were able to find People to help and he hoped that they were well. But he did not know where they were or how to find them.

Waaseyaa decided to walk south along the west shore of the great river known as Magtogoek, which, as I told you, was formed by the melting of the Ice Giants. Perhaps, Waaseyaa thought, he could find other People to help or maybe find one of his lost brothers and sisters.

After three nights and four days, Waaseyaa found an island with a village called Tiohtià:ke. The People in the village were happy to see Waaseyaa but they immediately asked for his help in rescuing a little girl who was trapped in a small cave.

Waaseyaa was glad to have the opportunity to serve and he bent down to see if he could go in and rescue the girl.

Waaseyaa realized that he was too large to fit into the cave and it was too dark for him to see the lost girl. He thought that if he had helpers, perhaps one of them would be small enough to go into the cave and rescue the little girl.

Waaseyaa remembered that the Creator gave him as a gift a share in the Creator's power to create other living beings. He decided to pray to the Creator that he would be able to call forth children of his own to help him free the lost girl.

The Creator, seeing that Waaseyaa was now separated from his brothers and sisters and that he needed help to rescue the girl, decided now was the time for Waaseyaa to use his gift to create a family of his own. The Creator explained to Waaseyaa that he could now create his own children by using objects scattered about in the World.

Looking around for something with which to create his first child, Waaseyaa found a log lying on the ground. He lifted it up and when he turned the log over, out popped his eldest daughter, Wowkwis the Fox.

Next, he picked up a piece of bark that he found next to the log. Waaseyaa threw the bark into the air towards Grandfather Sun. While still high in the sky, Grandfather Sun's fire burned the bark until it became black as coal. The burnt bark then transformed into his oldest son, Wiskijan the Raven.

Waaseyaa and his children returned to the People and offered to help. Seeing that his daughter Wowkwis the Fox was small enough to fit through the small opening to the cave, Waaseyaa asked her to go in and find the girl. Meanwhile, Wiskijan the Raven could fly far above the cave and look for another entrance so the People could reach the lost girl.

The cave was dark and frightening, but Wowkwis the Fox was brave, and she carefully crawled deeper into the cave. At last, she saw the little girl, holding her knees and weeping quietly.

After letting the girl know that she was now safe, Wowkwis the
Fox signaled to her brother Wiskijan the Raven. He then guided
the People to where they could throw a rope down to the lost girl
and pull her up to safety. Waaseyaa, Wowkwis and Wiskijan then
returned the girl to her grateful parents.

The Creator rewarded Wowkwis the Fox and her brother Wiskijan the Raven for their bravery. From that day forward, they helped their Father Waaseyaa as an Elder Sister and an Elder Brother of the People.

Mont-St Hilaire
Les Créateurs
Mont Orford
Lac Magog
Les frères & Sœurs
Bolton Centre
Mont Sutton
Lac Memphrémagog
De Waaseyaa & Mikcheech
Mikcheech
Le Géant de Montagne Tremblant
Fleuve Saint-Laurent
Québec
Waaseyaa
Memphré
Lac Memphrémagog

It was around this time that Waaseyaa would spend long moments wondering what happened to his sisters Wenona the Orca, Namid the Snowy Owl and Bawaajige the Polar Bear, and his brothers Shkaabewis the Caribou and Animkii the Bald Eagle.

On clear, dark nights, Waaseyaa would look up and ponder the stars. He wondered where his brothers and sisters were, and he found it comforting to imagine that they were also looking at the same stars at the same moment that he was.

Waaseyaa also worried about his brother Mikcheech and prayed to the Creator that he would be safe if Lugubre returned.

Because of these thoughts, Waaseyaa decided that he must not remain any longer with the People of the island but continue to travel the World with the hope of finding his lost brothers and sisters.

So, having already spent many years with the People of the island, Waaseyaa the Giant, his daughter Wowkwis the Fox and his son Wiskijan the Raven crossed the great river and headed east.

As they journeyed to the east, they crossed a vast open plain with large mountains scattered about like giants sleeping on the ground.

Waaseyaa was curious about the Mountain Giants because up to that time, he thought that he was the only giant in the World. He tried to talk to them and ask if his brothers and sisters had come this way. However, the giants' sleep was too deep for them to wake up and answer him. Therefore, Waaseyaa and his children continued on.

After two nights and three days, they arrived at a village on
the shore of Lake Memphrémagog at the foot of Mont-Orford.
Waaseyaa and his children could see that the People built homes
for themselves. However, there were no giants to talk to and his
brothers and sisters were nowhere to be found.

An elder villager approached them as they got closer.

"Welcome, Elder Brother," he said to Waaseyaa. "We know that the
Creator has sent you to help and teach us."

Waaseyaa noticed that the man was thin and weak.

"We will share what we have," the elder continued,
"but we don't have much."

As Waaseyaa looked around the village, he noticed that the villagers
were as listless as the elder.

"Have any of my brothers and sisters been here to help you?"
asked Waaseyaa.

"No," responded a woman elder, "no one has been here but you. We
need food, but none of the Elder Beings have visited us and taught
us how to feed ourselves."

"We feel forgotten," said another man. "Will you help us? Is that why
you have come?"

"We will help you!" Waaseyaa told the man.

Waaseyaa looked around the village and saw that it was true. The People did not know how to find food for themselves because none of his brothers and sisters had been here to teach them. Perhaps, Waaseyaa thought, he could create two new helpers who were skilled at finding food and could then teach the People to find food for themselves.

After praying to the Creator, Waaseyaa found two boulders on the shore of Lake Memphrémagog. Placing his hands on the boulders, they began to move and come to life under his touch. One boulder transformed into a bear that Waaseyaa named Muin, and the other boulder became a racoon he that he named Azeban.

Why did Waaseyaa create a bear and a raccoon? Because bears and racoons are always hungry, and they are clever in knowing where to find food.

Seeing that the People were hungry, Muin jumped into Lake Memphrémagog to catch some fish for them to eat while Azeban picked some delicious berries on the shore of the lake so that the People would be fed.

The People watched Muin and Azeban carefully. Then, following their example, they jumped into the lake to catch fish and helped Azeban pick some berries.

The lake, however, was inhabited by Memphré the Lake Monster.

Remember how I told you that after the Creator called forth Waaseyaa and his brothers and sisters that next came the giants that lived in the mountains and the Lake Monsters who guarded the lakes? Well, Memphré is the eldest sister of all the other Lake Monsters. She is as long as twenty canoes, and her neck and head can stand high out of the water as a giant sequoia tree is tall. Her mouth could swallow three of my fishing boats. She has other sisters who guard their own lakes. They are:

Ogopogo, who lives in Okanagan Lake in British Columbia.

Seelkee, who makes her home in the swamps of Chilliwack, also in British Columbia.

Next is Manipogo, who guards Lake Manitoba in Manitoba.

Out on Lake Superior, lives Memphré's sister Mishipeshu.

And Champ, the youngest of the Lake Monster Sisters, lives on Lake Champlain, which is shared between New York, Vermont and Québec.

Now, would you be frightened by such a large beast rising out
of the water? I know I would be, and just so, the People were
understandably frightened by Memphré because they had never
seen a creature like her before.

"Must we starve only to be eaten by this fearsome beast?" they cried
out as they tried to hide behind Waaseyaa.

However, as an Elder Being herself, Memphré the Lake Monster had
compassion for the People. Inspired by Muin's efforts, she gave them
fish that she had captured with her huge mouth. There were now
enough fish for them to eat, so that no one was hungry.

She only asked in return that the People allow her to live in peace in
Lake Memphrémagog at the foot of Mont-Orford.

The Creator rewarded Muin and Azeban for their cunning and resourcefulness, who, by their example, taught the People how to find food for themselves to eat.

The People also thanked Memphré the Lake Monster for her generosity in giving them enough fish so that they would not starve.

Muin and Azeban then joined their sister Wowkwis the Fox and their brother Wiskijan the Raven as helpers of their father, Waaseyaa.

After the Creator rewarded Muin and Azeban, Waaseyaa turned towards Memphré. He was happy to meet another Elder Being and seeing her reminded Waaseyaa how much he missed his own brothers and sisters. Waaseyaa hoped that now that the People had been fed, she could now help him find his lost brothers and sisters.

After thanking Memphré for helping the People, Waaseyaa described his brothers and sisters to her and explained how he and Mikcheech became separated from them soon after the creation of the World. Finally, he asked Memphré if she had seen them or could at least guide him to where they might be.

She said that she did not, however, she did know that far to the north there was a Trembling Mountain that was sacred to the People who lived there. On top of the sacred mountain, Memphré explained, there lived a giant who was even bigger than Waaseyaa. From the top of his mountain, this giant could see far over the whole World. Perhaps, she suggested, he may have seen Waaseyaa's lost brothers and sisters and could tell him where he could find them.

Waaseyaa wanted to meet this Mountain Giant and ask him about his brothers and sisters. So, with his children, he journeyed to the north towards the mountain.

After walking for as many days as the moon has in its cycle, Waaseyaa and his children arrived at a village at the base of the Trembling Mountain.

The People in the village said that the giant would sometimes shake his mountain to remind the People that he was watching them to ensure that they behave.

Upon seeing Waaseyaa, the Trembling Mountain Giant shook his mountain in greeting. However, the shaking caused a huge tree to land on a long house in the village, trapping a family inside.

Waaseyaa could see the People struggling to move the tree off the long house with the trapped family inside. He realized that perhaps he could call forth another helper who could help them with his strength and determination.

After praying to the Creator, Waaseyaa pulled down a branch from a nearby tree and created his youngest son, Puku'kowij the Moose. Waaseyaa then pointed to the fallen tree that had trapped the family and asked Puku'kowij if he would help the People and pull it off.

Using his great strength, Puku'kowij the Moose pulled the tree off the long house, freeing the trapped family.

The Creator rewarded Puku'kowij for his strength and determination. He joined his Elder Brothers Wiskijan, Muin, Azeban and his Elder Sister Wowkwis as helpers of their father, Waaseyaa the Giant.

Now that the family was rescued from the falling tree, Waaseyaa wanted to climb the Trembling Mountain and ask the giant if he had seen his brothers and sisters. But before Waaseyaa could begin to climb the mountain, the giant raised his arm and pointed towards something behind Waaseyaa.

Just as Waaseyaa turned to look to where the giant was pointing, he was surprised to hear someone call his name.

"Waaseyaa! We have been looking for you and Mikcheech since we lost you both at the beginning of the World."

The voice was familiar to Waaseyaa, but it was so long ago, was it possible? Could it be?

Waaseyaa saw a flash of white as something flew out of the forest.

Yes! It was his sister Namid the Snowy Owl that called his name. The long-lost brother and sister embraced.

Namid pointed at a wing back to the forest. "Look, Waaseyaa, I have brought everyone with me!"

Waaseyaa stared at the forest with wonder and joy as he saw his long-lost brothers and sisters stepping out of the forest.

First there was his sister Bawaajige the Polar Bear, and then his brothers Shkaabewis the Caribou and Animkii the Bald Eagle.

As Waaseyaa counted his brothers and sister, he became sad when he realized that sister Wenona the Orca was not there.

"Where is Wenona?" he asked. "Is she all right? And I wish Mikcheech could have been here to see all of you."

As if in response, Waaseyaa saw a great shadow of something large flying overhead. As he looked up, he saw Mikcheech waving to him, standing on the back of Wenona.

"Look who I have found, brother!" shouted Mikcheech as they flew by.

Seeing that everyone was finally reunited, Waaseyaa introduced his children to his brothers and sisters.

Waaseyaa asked his brother Animkii, "How did you know where to find me? I have been looking for all of you."

Animkii told Waaseyaa that while Waaseyaa was looking for them, they were all searching for him and Mikcheech. They too heard about the giant who lived on top of the Trembling Mountain and that from the top of his mountain he could see the whole World. They all arrived a few days earlier so they could meet with the giant and ask him if he had seen Waaseyaa and Mikcheech, and perhaps tell them where they could find their lost brothers.

The Mountain Giant told them that he could see Mikcheech living with the People in a village to the southeast, and that he could see Waaseyaa crossing the great river Magtogoek to the south and that he was walking towards the Trembling Mountain. The giant said that everyone was welcome to stay at his mountain and wait for Waaseyaa to arrive while Wenona volunteered to find Mikcheech.

After thanking the Mountain Giant, Wenona flew off to Trois Rivières and found Mikcheech exactly where the Mountain Giant said he would be. She brought Mikcheech back to the Trembling Mountain to join Namid, Bawaajige, Shkaabewis and Animkii while they waited for Waaseyaa.

Now that Waaseyaa had finally arrived with his children, his brothers and sisters came out to meet him.

The People were also happy for Waaseyaa and his family and together celebrated the joy of finding each other again.

The Creator was also pleased with Mikcheech, Memphré, Waaseyaa and his children, who used many different lessons to teach the People the way to live as the Creator had intended.

Waaseyaa showed the People how to be wise and how to build things like a home to live in and fires to keep them warm.

Mikcheech taught the People kindness and gave them stories to tell their grandchildren.

Wowkwis the Fox and Wiskijan the Raven demonstrated bravery.

Muin the Bear and Azeban the Racoon were clever and resourceful.

Memphré the Lake Monster gave the People an example of generosity.

Puku'kowij the Moose used strength and determination to persevere in the face of danger.

You will do well, my grandchildren, to follow their teachings and to tell their stories to your grandchildren, as I am doing for you.

Afterwards, Waaseyaa the Giant and his children Wowkwis, Wiskijan, Muin, Azeban and Puku'kowij returned to Mont-Orford and made their home there. They would often visit Mikcheech the Turtle at his pond at Trois Rivières or they would visit their aunts and uncles among the Elder Beings of the North lands.

Although Mikcheech would occasionally go on adventures with his niece and nephews near Mont-Orford, he would always return to his pond at Trois Rivières. Mikcheech loved the People of Trois Rivières, whom he saw as his children.

Of all his children at Trois Rivières, his dearest friend was an Algonquin girl named Miteouamigoukou, whom Mikcheech nicknamed Little Mischief. Who was Miteouamigoukou, you ask? Well, she is my Old Grandmother, and that means she is your Old Grandmother as well. Did she have magical adventures?
Oh, yes, she did!

But that is a story for another night, around another campfire.

Mont-St-Hilaire
Les Créateurs
Mont Orford
Lac Magog
Les frères & Sœurs
Bolton Centre
De Waaseyaa & Mikcheech
Mont Sutton
Lac Memphrémagog
Mikcheech
Le Géant de Montagne Tremblant
Fleuve Saint-Laurent
Québec
Waaseyaa
Memphré
Lac Memphrémagog

Mount Orford, Québec

March 5, 2064

OJIBWE
SKI RESORT
CoCoa
Petit...$
Moyen...$
Grand...$

Artist Statement
by Natasha Pelley-Smith

After the success of Volume 1 and Volume 2 of the *Old Grandmother's Tree* series, it's been incredibly heartwarming to see the support and joy the books have sparked in readers around the world. That's why I was so thrilled to continue this journey with author and co-creator Joseph Bolton through this new standalone installment: *Dance of Creation*.

For this book, I've remained true to the artistic style that shaped the series, while digitally illustrating a magical new chapter—one that reveals the origin story behind the beloved trickster animals and folklore introduced in the first two volumes.

Bringing this story to life has been a creative adventure of its own. I've continued to draw inspiration from Joe's vibrant storytelling, the influence of storyboard artist Masami, and my own personal connection to nature and real-life encounters with some of these animals. Together, these influences shaped the visual rhythm of this creation tale.

I hope readers feel the same sense of wonder and spirit that guided me throughout the illustration process. It's a joy to share *Dance of Creation* and invite you once again into the world of Old Grandmother's Tree.

On the summit of Mount Orford, Quebec
to observe the April 2024 total eclipse.

About the Author

Joseph Bolton was born in Pawtucket, Rhode Island, during the twilight of the golden age of French-Canadian culture in New England. Growing up immersed in his mother's French-Canadian family, Joseph enjoyed hearing the stories told by his grandparents and great aunts of a mysterious and magical place called Québec, otherwise known as "the place we came from."

After high school, Joseph's adventurous nature led him to enlist in the U.S. Army, and he served in the Army's airborne forces as a paratrooper jumping out of perfectly good airplanes, much to the worry of his mother.

Although he originally intended to stay in the Army for two years, he was appointed to the United States Military Academy at West Point, and after graduating in 1989, he decided to make the Army a career. After West Point, Joseph graduated from the Army's Ranger Training School, a grueling and physically demanding combat leadership course. Over the next 18 years, Joseph served in the army in various positions of growing responsibilities culminating with a combat tour in Afghanistan as one of two Space Operations Officers with the US Army's 10th Mountain Division.

Since he retired from the Army, Joseph has worked in various project manager roles as a civilian contractor for the U.S. Air Force. While writing *Old Grandmother's Tree*, Joseph took a sabbatical from the U.S. Air Force and taught mathematics to young students for a semester at Holy Family Academy in Gardner, Massachusetts. He considers it the most fulfilling job he has ever had and hopes to return to teaching full-time in the near future.

Bolton is of French-Canadian, Algonquin, Spanish, English, and Irish descent, and is profoundly inspired by the stories of his heritage. He lives with his wife in Massachusetts, and, in his free time, enjoys hiking and skiing through Québec and New England landscapes. His favorite places to go for outdoor adventure are the Berkshire Mountains of Massachusetts and Mont-Orford in Québec. When he is not writing, hiking, or skiing, Joseph enjoys reading about science, history, philosophy, mathematics, and worldwide mythologies. He has been featured on many podcasts in the United States and Canada, and Dance of Creation is the third volume of his acclaimed *Old Grandmother's Tree* book series.

Visit his website for future updates on the upcoming Volume 4 of *Old Grandmother's Tree*: www.oldgrandmotherstree.com

About the Illustrator

Natasha Pelley-Smith is a professional artist born in Toronto, Canada, and a graduate of the renowned Écohlcité Fine Arts Academy in France (now part of École Émile Cohl of Lyon), where she completed her training in 2017. Her artistic practice spans large-scale murals, illustrated books, and expressive canvas paintings using oils, acrylics, and mixed media—a testament to her versatility and deep creative roots.

Natasha's work is infused with the spirit of her heritage—Indigenous, Jamaican, and Newfoundland—as well as the cultural and educational influences gathered from her life and travels. Now back in Canada, she continues to make meaningful contributions to the art world through corporate, residential, commercial, and municipal art projects, as well as personal and collaborative illustration work.

Currently, Natasha remains immersed in illustrating the Old Grandmother's Tree series, bringing each page to life with care and imagination. To explore more of her art, visit:

welcome.natashapsartwork.ca

About the Storyboard Artist

Masami F. Kiyono is a biracial Japanese American Illustrator and Storyboard Artist who has worked on projects ranging from children's storybooks to Super Bowl commercials. One of her latest projects includes creating illustrations for a documentary titled Voices of Deoli (2024), which tells the story of how roughly 3,000 Chinese Indians were imprisoned in internment camps after the Sino-Indian War, and how the remaining survivors manage to thrive today.

In her free time, Masami enjoys watching cartoons and learning about folklore. These interests, along with her cultural background, influence her work, often containing dark whimsy and a bit of humor.

For the third installment in the *Old Grandmother's Tree* series, Masami and Joseph collaborated once more to tell the story of the origin of Miteouamigoukoue's world.

The Meunier family's adventures begin.

VOLUME I

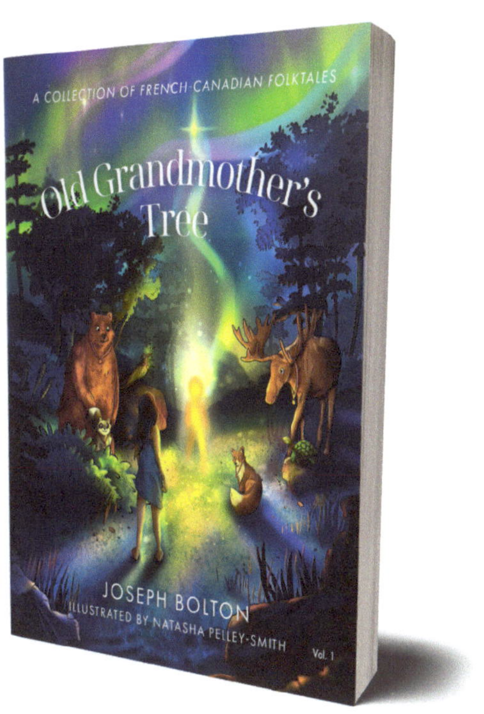

A history of family connections, cunning trickster animals, and adventures untold: *Old Grandmother's Tree: A Collection of French-Canadian Folktales* is a beautiful compilation of folktales set against the backdrop of 17th and early 20th century Québec.

On her wedding night, a young Algonquin woman is visited by the spirit of her first husband and the trickster animals of Indigenous legends, who encourage her to set forth on a new journey. So begins the Meunier family's origin story and the many adventures that come through the generations that follow.

Combining richly woven stories and stunning artwork, Joseph Bolton's and Natasha Pelley-Smith's *Old Grandmother's Tree* is a tribute to an untold history that will touch any reader.

VOLUME II

A history of family connections, cunning trickster animals, and adventures untold; the second volume of *Old Grandmother's Tree: A Collection of French-Canadian Folktales* expands the beautiful compilation of folktales seen in volume one, set against the backdrop of early 20th century Québec.

On a frosty autumn morning in 1902, lumberjack Jacques LaRue enthralls the Meunier family with a strange tale of a mysterious forest giant inhabiting the slopes of Mont-Orford. So begins the next installment of the Meunier family's adventures as they navigate a world of ancient trickster animals and family connections.

Combining richly woven stories and stunning artwork, Joseph Bolton's and Natasha Pelley-Smith's *Old Grandmother's Tree* is a tribute to an untold history that will touch any reader.

www.ingramcontent.com/pod-product-compliance
Lightning Source LLC
Chambersburg PA
CBHW041423300726
48981CB00007B/391